f

I Have A Weird Brother Who Digested A Fly

BOY

MOUTH

FLY

GALLBLADDER

ESOPHAGUS

LIVER

STOMACH

LARGE INTESTINE

SMALL INTESTINE

PANCREAS

RECTUM

Joan Holub AUTHOR

ILLUSTRATOR Patrick Girouard

Albert Whitman & Company, Morton Grove, Illinois

Thanks to Robert Chamovitz, M.D., for his help.

Library of Congress Cataloging-in-Publication Data

Holub, Jean.
I have a weird brother who digested a fly / by Jean Holub ;
illustrated by Patrick Girouard.
p. cm.
Summary: Illustrations and a humorous rhyme describe what happens when a
boy swallows a fly. Presents factual information about the digestive system.
ISBN 0-8075-3506-0
1. Digestion—Juvenile literature. [1. Digestion. 2. Digestive system.]
I. Girouard, Patrick, ill. II. Title.
QP145.H57 1999
612.3—dc21 99-12389
CIP

The art is rendered in ink, markers, gouache, and colored pencil.
The display type is set in Lambada.
The text type is set in Fenteen.
The design is by Scott Piehl.

For my brother, Paul.

—J. H.

For Sandra Kay,
who planted the seed.

—P. G.

I have a weird brother
who swallowed a fly.
In the blink of an eye,
he swallowed that fly.

I wonder why?

The fly floated.
It splashed.
It did the backstroke.

Before your body can use food, it
must change it into very tiny bits that
your blood can carry throughout your
body. This process, called digestion,
starts in the mouth.

My brother turned green and let out a croak.

Saliva (or spit) is watery stuff in your mouth that helps begin this change. It has chemicals called enzymes (EHN-zyms) that start to break the food down. Saliva also wets the food so it is easier to chew and swallow.

Sniff a juicy orange. Does your mouth water? That means saliva is coming out of small openings under your tongue and in your cheeks.

The fly wiggle-woggled around in his mouth, bumping his teeth before moving south.

Teeth also help break food into smaller pieces. Chew some celery 20 times. What change did chewing make in the celery?

Your tongue moves the food so your teeth can chew it. It pushes the food toward the back of your mouth to help you swallow. Little bumps on your tongue called taste buds help you taste bitter, sour, salty, and sweet flavors.

Gulp! So long, fly!
That fly headed inside.
It swished down a tube
on a wild water slide.

Your throat squeezes together when you swallow. It pushes the food down into a tube called the esophagus (ee-SAHF-uh-guhs). The esophagus connects your throat to your stomach. Food does not drop down this tube. It is squeezed along by muscles just as toothpaste is squeezed from a tube. You don't have to think about this. It simply happens.

It got squashed and squeezed
into yucky fly goop.
It got mixed and mashed
till it turned into soup.

Food reaches your stomach next. Your stomach is like a balloon that will stretch to hold food. It can hold about 4 cups at a time. It has muscles that mash and stir the food and push it farther along on its trip. It also has enzymes and acids that break food down even more. Food stays in your stomach until it turns into a kind of soup. This takes about 3 hours.

The fly whooshed through a tunnel,
back and forth, side to side.

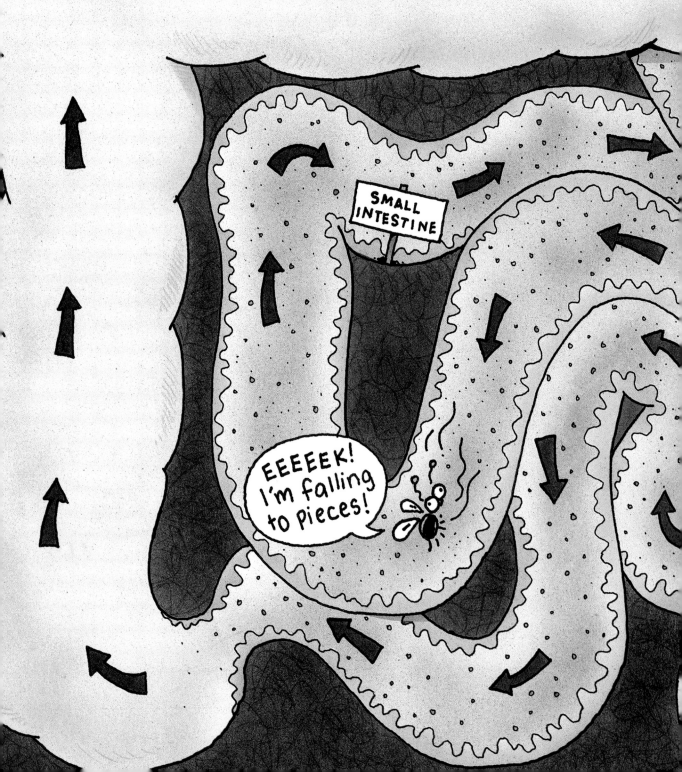

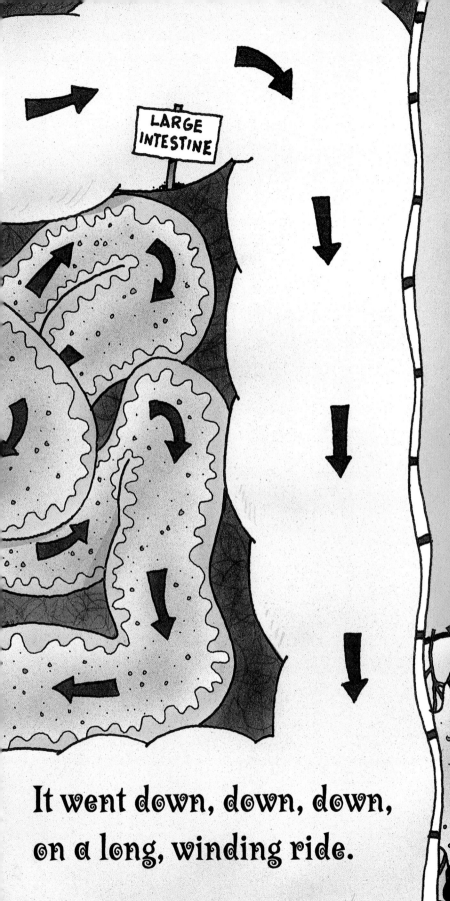

LARGE INTESTINE

It went down, down, down, on a long, winding ride.

Next the mushy food is squeezed through a tube called the small intestine, which is about 20 feet long. How can a tube that long fit inside you? It winds back and forth.

In the small intestine, food is mixed with enzymes and other chemicals. Some of these come from your nearby liver, gallbladder, and pancreas. These chemicals break the food into pieces so tiny you can't even see them.

Useful food parts are now little enough to pass from your small intestine into your blood. Blood carries them all around your body. Food parts that are not useful pass into the large intestine.

TINY FOOD PIECES

BLOOD VESSELS

After twenty-four hours
(it took a whole day!),
the fly turned into waste...

The parts of the food that cannot be changed so your body can use them are called waste. If you really ate a fly, some of it would be used by your body. The rest would become waste.

In the large intestine, a tube about 5 feet long, waste loses water and becomes solid. It is stored in your rectum, the end part of your large intestine, until you go to the bathroom.

My brother turned cartwheels—
at least ten or so.
Where did he find
all his get-up-and-go?

Just like a car needs gas to go, your body needs food for energy. Food is the fuel that helps you run, think, and grow. It keeps every part of your body strong and alive. There are many different healthy foods, including milk products, meats, fish, vegetables, fruits, breads, cereals, and fats.

I have a weird brother who swallowed a fly. In the blink of an eye, he swallowed that fly.

I wonder why.

Well,

    maybe,

        perhaps,

he swallowed that fly…

Should I Eat a Fly?

No! Flies have sticky feet, so they pick up lots of yucky stuff. They can carry diseases.

Gotta Go!

Your 2 kidneys remove waste and water from your blood to form urine. The urine is stored in your bladder. Because your bladder can only hold up to 2 cups of urine at a time, you have to urinate several times each day.

Smelly Food

Hold your nose and close your eyes. Ask a friend to give you some food. Can you guess what the food is? It's not easy! Your senses of taste and smell work together. That's why when your nose is stopped up, your food doesn't taste as good.

Funny Noises

You swallow air along with your food. Small amounts of air may come back up from your stomach as a burp. In some countries, people think it's good manners to burp after a meal: a burp means you liked the food.

Most of waste is solid, but a small part is gas. Occasionally some gas passes from the rectum as a noise. It often smells bad. This gas is called flatus (FLAY-tuhs); when it leaves your body, you are "passing gas."

What Do Bugs Taste Like?

Some bugs taste yummy when cooked properly and mixed with other ingredients. Stinkbugs are said to taste like apples. Some spiders taste like peanut butter. Ants taste a bit sweet.

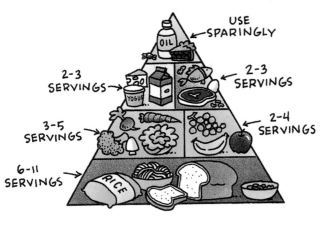

The Food Pyramid

The U.S. Department of Agriculture created the Food Guide Pyramid to help people choose the right amounts of healthy foods to eat each day. You should eat less of the foods at the the top of the pyramid and more of those at the bottom.

Small or Large?

Your small intestine isn't really small. It's a thin tube approximately 20 feet long in a grownup. That's about as long as 1 1/2 cars! The large intestine is only about 5 feet long. So why is it called the "large" intestine? Because it's about 2 1/2 inches wide. That's much wider than the small intestine, which is a little more than 1 inch wide.

Chomp, Chomp!

You will eat about 35 tons of food during your lifetime. That's as much as 12 very large hippos weigh!

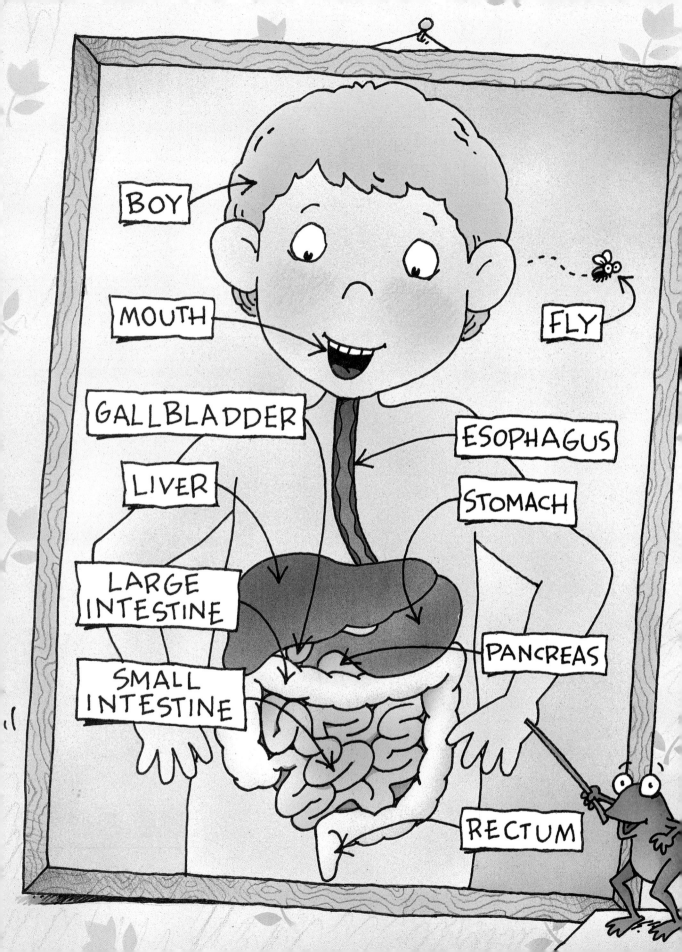

...it got flushed away.

My brother turned cartwheels—
at least ten or so.
Where did he find
all his get-up-and-go?

Just like a car needs gas to go, your body needs food for energy. Food is the fuel that helps you run, think, and grow. It keeps every part of your body strong and alive. There are many different healthy foods, including milk products, meats, fish, vegetables, fruits, breads, cereals, and fats.

I have a weird brother
who swallowed a fly.
In the blink of an eye,
he swallowed that fly.

I wonder why.

Well,
    maybe,
        perhaps,

he swallowed that fly...

Should I Eat a Fly?

No! Flies have sticky feet, so they pick up lots of yucky stuff. They can carry diseases.

Gotta Go!

Your 2 kidneys remove waste and water from your blood to form urine. The urine is stored in your bladder. Because your bladder can only hold up to 2 cups of urine at a time, you have to urinate several times each day.

Smelly Food

Hold your nose and close your eyes. Ask a friend to give you some food. Can you guess what the food is? It's not easy! Your senses of taste and smell work together. That's why when your nose is stopped up, your food doesn't taste as good.

Funny Noises

You swallow air along with your food. Small amounts of air may come back up from your stomach as a burp. In some countries, people think it's good manners to burp after a meal: a burp means you liked the food.

Most of waste is solid, but a small part is gas. Occasionally some gas passes from the rectum as a noise. It often smells bad. This gas is called flatus (FLAY-tuhs); when it leaves your body, you are "passing gas."

What Do Bugs Taste Like?

Some bugs taste yummy when cooked properly and mixed with other ingredients. Stinkbugs are said to taste like apples. Some spiders taste like peanut butter. Ants taste a bit sweet.

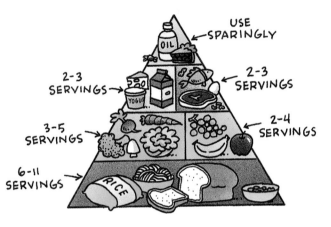

The Food Pyramid

The U.S. Department of Agriculture created the Food Guide Pyramid to help people choose the right amounts of healthy foods to eat each day. You should eat less of the foods at the the top of the pyramid and more of those at the bottom.

Small or Large?

Your small intestine isn't really small. It's a thin tube approximately 20 feet long in a grownup. That's about as long as 1 1/2 cars! The large intestine is only about 5 feet long. So why is it called the "large" intestine? Because it's about 2 1/2 inches wide. That's much wider than the small intestine, which is a little more than 1 inch wide.

Chomp, Chomp!

You will eat about 35 tons of food during your lifetime. That's as much as 12 very large hippos weigh!

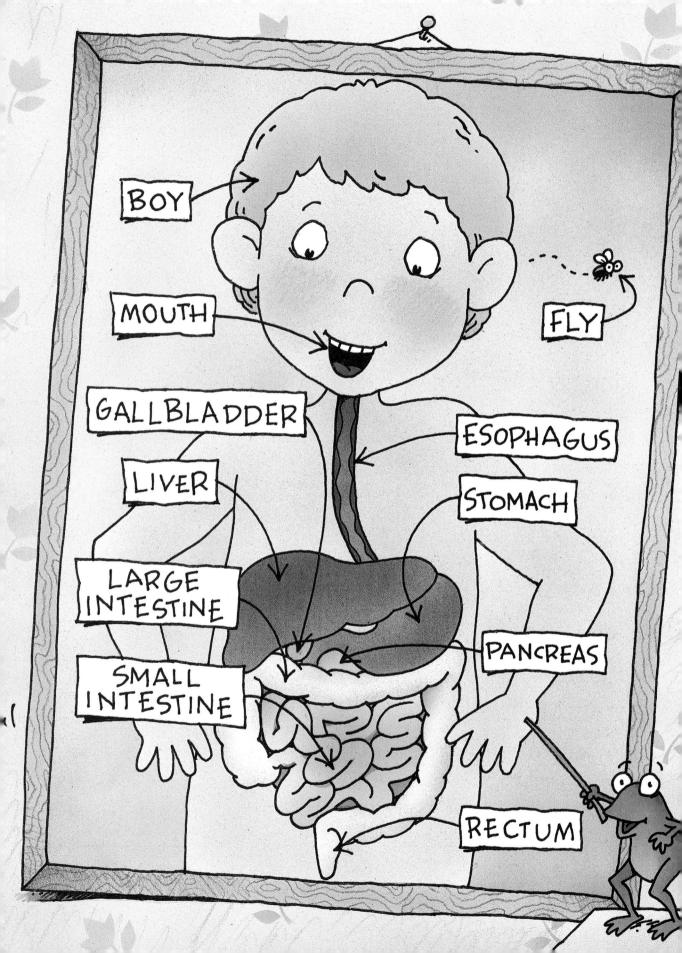

My brother turned cartwheels—
at least ten or so.
Where did he find
all his get-up-and-go?

Just like a car needs gas to go, your body needs food for energy. Food is the fuel that helps you run, think, and grow. It keeps every part of your body strong and alive. There are many different healthy foods, including milk products, meats, fish, vegetables, fruits, breads, cereals, and fats.

I have a weird brother
who swallowed a fly.
In the blink of an eye,
he swallowed that fly.

I wonder why.

Well,
    maybe,
        perhaps,
he swallowed that fly...

Should I Eat a Fly?

No! Flies have sticky feet, so they pick up lots of yucky stuff. They can carry diseases.

Gotta Go!

Your 2 kidneys remove waste and water from your blood to form urine. The urine is stored in your bladder. Because your bladder can only hold up to 2 cups of urine at a time, you have to urinate several times each day.

Smelly Food

Hold your nose and close your eyes. Ask a friend to give you some food. Can you guess what the food is? It's not easy! Your senses of taste and smell work together. That's why when your nose is stopped up, your food doesn't taste as good.

Funny Noises

You swallow air along with your food. Small amounts of air may come back up from your stomach as a burp. In some countries, people think it's good manners to burp after a meal: a burp means you liked the food.

Most of waste is solid, but a small part is gas. Occasionally some gas passes from the rectum as a noise. It often smells bad. This gas is called flatus (FLAY-tuhs); when it leaves your body, you are "passing gas."

What Do Bugs Taste Like?

Some bugs taste yummy when cooked properly and mixed with other ingredients. Stinkbugs are said to taste like apples. Some spiders taste like peanut butter. Ants taste a bit sweet.

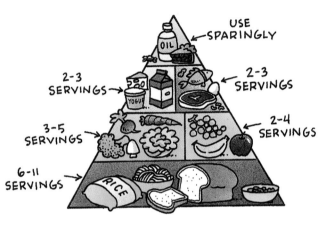

The Food Pyramid

The U.S. Department of Agriculture created the Food Guide Pyramid to help people choose the right amounts of healthy foods to eat each day. You should eat less of the foods at the the top of the pyramid and more of those at the bottom.

Small or Large?

Your small intestine isn't really small. It's a thin tube approximately 20 feet long in a grownup. That's about as long as 1 1/2 cars! The large intestine is only about 5 feet long. So why is it called the "large" intestine? Because it's about 2 1/2 inches wide. That's much wider than the small intestine, which is a little more than 1 inch wide.

Chomp, Chomp!

You will eat about 35 tons of food during your lifetime. That's as much as 12 very large hippos weigh!

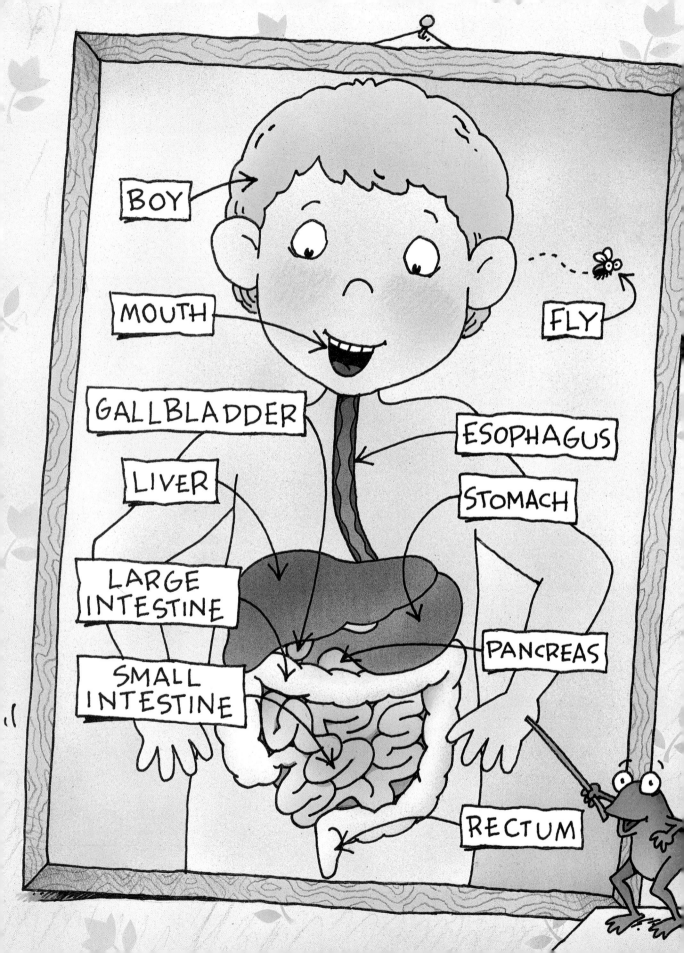